Tales
from
the BOX

The Countess's Calamity

For Lydia, with thanks for your help and support – love Mum

Published by Bloomsbury, New York and London
Distributed to the trade by Holtzbrinck Publishers

Library of Congress Cataloging-in-Publication Data
Gardner, Sally.   The Countess's calamity /
Sally Gardner. p. cm.
Summary: Five dolls, abandoned in a park, are
rescued by Mr. and Mrs. Mouse, who provide
a home for them and protect them through
various adventures despite the horrible
behavior of the doll called the Countess.
ISBN hc 1-58234-812-X (alk. Paper)
ppk 1-58234-855-3
[1. Dolls—Fiction. 2. Mice—Fiction. 3.
Parks—Fiction. 4. Behavior—Fiction.] I. Title.
PZ7.G179335 Co 2003   [Fic]—dc 21
2002028014

First U.S. Edition 2003
10 9 8 7 6 5 4 3 2 1

Bloomsbury USA
Children's Books
175 Fifth Avenue
New York, New York
10010

The Countess's Calamity

Sally Gardner

BLOOMSBURY
CHILDREN'S
BOOKS

chapter one

This is a story of five little dolls who
were left in a box, under a chair, in a park.
Why they were left there, I haven't a clue.
How long had they been there? I don't
rightly know. It couldn't have been long,
for this park is busy, with a bandstand,
a puppet theatre, a fountain and a café.

 On the day this story starts no one came
to collect the box. A dog sniffed at it but,
smelling nothing tasty, lost interest and
wandered off.

An elderly lady sat down on the chair, warming her face in the sun. Perhaps it is her box? Maybe she will remember it in a minute and pick it up. But no, as she got up to leave, her ebony walking stick pushed the box out of the way and under a bush.

It was getting late and people were going home. The park keeper closed the gates

and only the hum of the city could
be heard in the distance.

Everything became very quiet. A couple
of retired mice had their home under the
bush and were most surprised, not to say
a little put out, to find a box blocking
their front door.

'Well, what a business,' said Mr Mouse
when he finally managed to push the box
out of the way.

For this was the time of day when
Mr and Mrs Mouse collected their food.
The legs, you see, leave so much litter
behind them that every night there is a
feast to be found. But a box, now there's
a surprise!

'Maybe, my dear,' said Mrs Mouse,
'we will not need to travel far tonight
for it seems that our supper has been
delivered straight to the front door.'

Mr Mouse sniffed and twitched his
whiskers. 'It doesn't smell like food,'
he said, going back indoors.

He brought out a ladder and propped
it against the side of the box.

'Shall I see what's inside,
my little ribbly rodent?'
he said to his wife.

'Oh do,' giggled Mrs Mouse.

Mr Mouse climbed up the ladder,
gingerly lifted the lid and peeped inside.

'Go on, tell me what's in there,'
said Mrs Mouse. 'Not kittens I hope!'
she said, suddenly looking frightened.

'No, no,' said Mr Mouse. 'I think there
are clothes and things in here. I can
spy hats and shiny
shoes. Not on
anyone's feet
so to squeak.'

Mrs Mouse did a little dance.
'Oh my, how I would love
a new hat and new shoes,'
she sang.

'Then, my ribbly rodent, the love
of my whiskers, I will get you a new hat,'
said Mr Mouse and he began to climb
down into the box.

'If you are sure it's not kittens,
I'm coming too,' said Mrs Mouse.

chapter two

The dolls had all been jiggled
and joggled about. They were not
quite sure how long they had been
in the box or what to do about it.

'Maybe we're in an attic,' said
Quilt the sailor doll, 'and will
be brought out again later.'

'Why would anyone put us
in a box?' said the Countess.
'We are not baubles to be put
in an attic and forgotten. I am
from the Land of Lounge.
I have a red-plush chair
and a silver tea service. I don't
belong in a box being sniffed
at by goodness knows what.'

'I think,' said Ting Tang, a little cloth
doll with rosy cheeks and a smiling face,
'that it might have something to do with
the word birthday.'

'What does that mean?' said Boolar,
a handsome doll wearing a smart suit
and waistcoat.

'I believe it is a magic word,' said the
Countess. 'If I remember rightly, it brings
presents, like my silver tea service.'

'Or darkness like this box,'
said Quilt.

'Maybe,' said a small
boy doll called Stitch,
'*we* are the present and
we are going to a brand
new dolls' house.'

'Why of course,'
cried the Countess

with joy. 'That's it. Why didn't I think
of that? We are the birthday present.
Any minute now we will see the smiling
faces of happy children looking down at us.'

'Then why aren't we wrapped up in tissue
paper?' said Ting Tang.

'Simple,' replied the Countess. 'Whoever
is going to give us away was in such a
hurry they forgot.'

At that moment, the lid of the box was lifted off and the bewhiskered face of Mr Mouse peered down at them. All the dolls lay very still. 'You know,' said Mrs Mouse, looking about, 'there are dolls in here, as well as all these clothes and hats.' She went and looked at each doll carefully.

'They are very beautiful. Odd they should be left here and forgotten, don't you think?'

'It's a good thing they're not puppets,' said Mr Mouse, picking up a walking stick, 'otherwise we would be in trouble.'

'They do have some lovely things,' said Mrs Mouse, trying on a pair of shiny red shoes, then putting a large hat on her head.

'Don't I look a picture!'

'Put those back this instant! They don't belong to you,' said the Countess, trying to pull herself up on her china feet.

Mrs Mouse dropped the hat and ran to Mr Mouse. Holding onto him tightly, she squeaked, 'I thought you said they weren't puppets!'

Boolar stood up, followed by the others. 'What are you doing in our box?' he asked the mice.

'More to the point, what is your box doing, blocking our front door?' said Mr Mouse, sticking out his roly-poly tummy.

'Go away! Shoo!' said the Countess. 'We are an important birthday present.'

Mrs Mouse started to giggle.
'Pardon my whiskers, but it's rather
strange, don't you think, to put a
birthday present under a bush in a park?'

'So we are not in an attic,' said Quilt sadly.

'Certainly not,' said Mr Mouse. 'Why,
I have a cousin who lives in an attic. A
horrible place. No fresh air, lots of dust
and, more to the point, hardly any food.
As thin as a slice of cheese is my cousin.
Not like us,' added Mr Mouse, patting
his round furry tummy.

'Are you sure we are in a park?'
asked Boolar. 'Do you mean
we are out in the open
where it rains and the
wind blows?'

'Well, it can do those things.
But we live under an evergreen

bush which helps,'
said Mr Mouse.

'What's that?' asked Ting Tang.

'A bush that never loses its leaves,'
explained Mr Mouse.

'Our home is snug and warm with
all mod cons,' added Mrs Mouse.

'Oh, really,' said the Countess, stamping
her foot. 'This is too much. Will you
kindly go away,' she said, trying to shoo
Mr and Mrs Mouse out of the box.
'Put the wrapping paper back
as you found it. We will be
collected shortly and no one
wants to receive a scrunched-
up present.'

Mr and Mrs Mouse huffed
and left, muttering to
themselves that outside

their front door was a very unusual place to put a present. The dolls lay down and waited, hoping the Countess was right and that at any moment they would be rescued. The darkness seemed to be getting thicker around them as they listened to the strange and frightening noises of the world outside.

'I don't like this,' whispered Ting Tang.

'It doesn't sound like an inside kind of place, does it,' said Quilt.

'I can feel my stuffing going all lumpy,' said Stitch.

'This isn't right,' said Boolar, getting up. 'I'm going to take a look outside and see what's going on.'

'No, don't!' the others cried.

'Just lie down again,' said the Countess.

'I tell you there is no need to panic.
At any moment the wrapping paper
will be torn off and we will be safe.'

'I've been thinking,' said Quilt. 'If there
was wrapping paper, wouldn't those mice
have had a lot more trouble lifting the lid
of our box?'

'Don't think. Just be still,' said the
Countess angrily.

Boolar ignored her and climbed up and
out of the box. What he saw made him
realise how small and lost they truly were.

It seemed to be getting darker by the second, as if a magician had thrown his cloak over the ground and was stealing the light away. Boolar climbed back into the box. All the dolls were sitting up now, apart from the Countess who lay there, stiff and proud, refusing to move.

'Tell us,' said Ting Tang, 'is there wrapping paper?'

'No,' said Boolar. 'I'm afraid the mice were right. We are under a bush.'

Stitch began to cry. 'I want to go home to my room with the painted walls and the rocking horse that goes to and fro,' he sobbed. Ting Tang put an arm round him. 'We all want to go home but we don't know how,' she said.

'We can't stay here,' said Quilt. 'I think we should see if Mr and Mrs Mouse can help.'

chapter three

The night air was chilly and damp. Boolar
was pleased to find a lantern hanging
above Mr and Mrs Mouse's front door.
He rang the bell hard.

Mr Mouse, dressed in a smoking jacket
and hat, opened it almost immediately.

'Good evening to you,' he said.
'Everything tickety-tails?'

'No,' said Boolar. 'I'm sorry to say we
all feel rather lost and frightened.'

'Mrs Mouse!' shouted Mr Mouse down
the long hall, 'we have guests for supper.'

'Are you sure?' said Boolar. 'I think we
may have been a little rude earlier.'

'Think nothing of it. Quite understandable.
Now go and get the others. Here,' said
Mr Mouse, handing Boolar the ladder,

'this will make it easier
to get up and down.'

'Thank you,' said Boolar.

Everyone was delighted,
everyone that is except
the Countess, who refused to move.

'Come on,' said Boolar. 'You can't stay
here all alone. I think we could do with
some food before our stuffing goes
limp, don't you?'

'If you expect someone of my
importance,' said the Countess with her
eyes closed, 'to leave a perfectly good
birthday present to go and eat with two
thieving good-for-nothing mice then you
are very much mistaken.'

Boolar sighed. 'We are not anyone's present, Countess,' he said sadly. 'We have been left out in a park, and I don't know why.' The Countess didn't move.

'Have it your own way,' said Boolar, carefully putting the lid back on as he left.

Mrs Mouse had laid the table with a feast of food. The four dolls had never seen anything like it. There were pies, cheeses, plates of salami, sausages, chips, little loaves of freshly baked bread, jelly, ice-cream and cherry tart, as well as a large jug of home-made lemonade. At the end

of the room a fire burned merrily in a
little grate. Mrs Mouse seemed worried
that there wasn't more to eat.

'Oh dear,' she said, 'do forgive me. If
I had known we were going to have guests
I would have made something special.'

'It is all quite wonderful,' said Boolar,
helping himself to seconds. 'It is a banquet
and far more tasty than dolls'-house food.'

'Hear, hear,' cried the other dolls.

By the end of the meal they were all so
full their stuffing hurt.

'I thank you from the last thread in my heart. We have been washed away by your kindness,' said Quilt. The other dolls agreed, lifting their glasses of lemonade to toast Mr and Mrs Mouse. It was such a jolly little party they had quite forgotten the Countess. That is, until the doorbell started to ring and ring and ring.

'Oh, bother my whiskers. Who can that be at this time of night?' said Mr Mouse, scurrying up the hall.

Mr Mouse came back with his paw around the Countess. She looked limp and pale and very unsteady on her feet. Boolar rushed to help. They propped her up on a chair at the end of the table.

'Oh my tail,' said Mrs Mouse, 'she doesn't look right.'

The dolls all gathered round.

'Stand back,' said Quilt. 'Let's give the Countess some air. Come on, stand back.'

Mr Mouse brought a glass of lemonade, and after a few sips the Countess recovered enough to speak. As the lamps

flickered low, sending large shadows over
the walls, she told them what had happened.

'I was attacked,' she said, 'by a cat of
monstrous size. It had a pointy nose
and ears, sharp white teeth and yellow eyes.
Its fur was mangy.'

Mrs Mouse squeaked. 'Are you sure the
front door is properly bolted?'

'It is, my ribbly rodent, it is,' said Mr Mouse.

The Countess continued. 'The horrid
creature put its face right into the
box and tried to catch hold of me.
I only just managed to escape.

It isn't right. We shouldn't be here,' she said.

Ting Tang patted her hand. 'Don't worry,' she said. 'We are safe with Mr and Mrs Mouse.'

The Countess's story had taken all the fun out of the little party, and they helped Mrs Mouse tidy up without saying another word.

'Well, that settles it. My whiskers tell me you will be staying here tonight,' said Mr Mouse. He led the dolls down a corridor lined with pictures of baby mice to a large clean room filled with seven beds.

'This is where my little ones used to sleep before they left home,' said Mr Mouse. 'The beds are clean and dry. Not dolls'- house standard but better, I hope. Goodnight, sleep tight.'

The dolls took off their shoes and coats and lay down on the soft feather mattresses. Even the Countess had to agree with Mr Mouse – they were very comfy beds indeed. It didn't take long before they were all fast asleep.

chapter four

'Tell us about the Land of Park,' said
Boolar to Mr Mouse over breakfast the
next day. They were sitting outside in the
early morning sunshine. Mrs Mouse had
brought out warm rolls and there was jam
and butter.

The box stood a little way off, undamaged
by whatever monster the Countess had
seen the night before.

Mr Mouse lit his pipe and sat back.
'The park is vast,' he began, spreading
his arms. 'It is a place where there is food
aplenty but also a place where you have to
be very, very careful. There are the puppets.'

'Do you mean dolls like us?'
interrupted Ting Tang.

'Not quite,' said Mr Mouse.

'They're not dolls'-house dolls. They are very big and grand and act in the puppet theatre. They are the stars of the park.'

'Do they twinkle?' asked Stitch.

'No,' laughed Mr Mouse. 'They're not those kind of stars. Sometimes we have travelling dolls who come to the puppet theatre, some with strings, some without. Then there are the mice like us. I have quite a few relations here in the park.'

'Warn them about Mr Cuddles,' said Mrs Mouse anxiously, as she brought out a jug of piping hot chocolate.

'I'm coming to him, the love of my whiskers,' said Mr Mouse. 'The park is home to a family of foxes. There are birds, bees, ducks, squirrels and, of course, the legs. But the one you must be on the look out for is Mr Cuddles the cat.

He is truly terrifying and belongs to the park keeper.'

Here, Mr Mouse paused. 'I think he may have been the one the Countess saw last night. He is, without doubt, the meanest, nastiest cat I have ever known. Why, only last year my wife lost her mother and father plus a collection of aunts, two uncles and one small but not forgotten cousin to that fiend.'

Mrs Mouse dabbed her eyes with a handkerchief. 'It has been very hard for my side of the family,' she said.

'I am most sorry to hear that,' said Quilt.

'Well,' said Mr Mouse. 'No good remembering sad things. I'm just telling you so that you're careful, that's all.'

The Countess dabbed her mouth with a napkin and stood up. 'None of this concerns us. Thank you for your kindness but now we must be getting along.'

'But why? You are most welcome to stay,' said Mr Mouse.

'It is quite simple,' said the Countess. 'Whoever was foolish enough to leave us here will be back for us today. Come along. There isn't a minute to lose.'

The other dolls didn't know what to do. They all felt rather anxious as they said farewell to Mr and Mrs Mouse.

'Where are we going?' asked Stitch.

'Back to the box,' said the Countess firmly.

chapter five

By the time the park keeper opened the gates that morning the box was again back under a chair with the dolls safely inside. Unlike the day before, they could now recognise every sound around them. The twittering of birds, crunching on the gravel, the scuff of a ball.

Suddenly, in one glorious heart-stopping moment, they felt themselves being lifted up in the air. The lid of the box was taken off by a little girl with curly hair.

'Mummy!' she shouted. 'Look what I've found. It's a box with tiny dolls in it.'

'What did I tell you?' whispered the Countess. 'I feel we are going home.'

'Chloe!' came the angry voice of a mother as the lid was snapped back on the box. 'How many times have I told you not to play with rubbish?'

The dolls felt themselves lifted up again as the box was propelled through the air.

'But, Mummy, they're dolls,' followed the disappointed voice of Chloe.

There was a thud as the box landed on something hard. The dolls were thrown higgledy-piggledy together in a corner of the upturned box.

'I should think we are nearly home now,' said the Countess, removing an umbrella that was sticking into her side.

'What makes you think that?' said Ting Tang. 'We have stopped moving.'

'You really are a cloth brain,' snapped the Countess. 'That's because we are in a shopping basket.'

The dolls heard another dull thud on the top of the box and had the sensation of sliding. As they did so, the lid of the box shifted slightly so that a small shaft of sunlight shone in.

'I'm sure we are in a shopping basket. I'm right,' snapped the Countess. 'You see, we are going home.'

Boolar untangled himself and looked out. All he could see was a thick green plastic curtain. All he could hear was the hum of bees. Boolar was unsure what a shopping basket looked like, but he had a nasty feeling that this wasn't one.

chapter six

The bees had told Mr and Mrs Mouse
that the box with the dolls inside had
been thrown away. There wasn't a minute
to lose, for it was well known to all who
lived in the park that the keeper emptied
the rubbish bins every evening. This
meant that whatever had been thrown
away that day would be gone for good.

It was hard at such short notice to put
together a rescue team. The
only help Mr Mouse
managed to get was the
old carrier pigeon who

said he would do any fetching needed.

'This is a proper pickle and no mistake,' said Mr Mouse as he climbed down into the rubbish bin. He had to move an old trainer and a banana skin before he could see the box.

'Hello, is anyone there?' he shouted.

'Yes,' called out Quilt. 'Mr Mouse, is that you?'

'Oh dear, you dolls are going to be the end of me,' said Mr Mouse, peering in at them. 'Come on, there isn't a

minute to lose. We have to get you out
of here before the park keeper catches us.'

'Thank you,' said the Countess
grandly. 'But we don't need your
help. You see, we are in this shopping
basket because we are going home.'

'No you're not,' said Mr Mouse
firmly. 'Shiver my whiskers,
you are in a rubbish
bin about to be
thrown away.'
He tried with all his
might to push the lid
further off the box.
Suddenly, he stopped
and put a paw to his ear.

'Listen,' he said.
'Can you hear that?'

The park keeper was doing his evening rounds, pushing his rattling cart with its wonky wheel down the gravel paths. He was on the look out for lost toys to add to the collection of dolls and teddies pinned to the front of his cart. They were grim reminders to children of what would happen if they were foolish enough to leave a beloved bear behind.

Usually, his cat, Mr Cuddles, kept the

park keeper company, ready
to pounce on anything they found
on their way. But this evening,
Mr Cuddles was curled up at home.
The park keeper sang in a deep
gruff voice.

'Three blind mice,
See how they run,
They all ran after the park keeper
Who knocked them down flat
With his leaf sweeper...'

As he sang, the park keeper laughed
wheezily and took out a big broom
from the front of his cart.

'Quick! Oh, my twirling tail,'
whispered Mr Mouse. 'There
isn't a moment to be lost.
He's nearly upon us.'

'Those three blind mice...'

The park keeper was getting closer.
Mr Mouse hurried the dolls out of the
box. Quilt took Ting Tang's hand and
Ting Tang held on tight to Stitch, Boolar
followed behind, while Mr Mouse waited
for the Countess, who wouldn't leave
the box no matter what.

'Come on,' urged Mr Mouse,
desperately tapping his foot.

'I'm not leaving,' said the Countess
stubbornly, holding on to her umbrella.
'This is where we belong.'

Boolar left the others and went back to
Mr Mouse to see what the trouble was.
Mr Mouse shrugged his shoulders.
'She won't budge,' he said.
'You go,' said Boolar.
'Mrs Mouse will be
getting worried. We'll

be along in a minute.'

'Oh dear, what a pickle,' said Mr Mouse, climbing as fast as his tummy would let him out of the bin and to safety.

'Look here,' said Boolar, 'if you don't come now, we will be thrown away with the rubbish. You don't want that, do you?'

'You go if you like,' said the Countess. 'I'm staying.'

'Please,' said Boolar who knew time was running out. 'For my sake, come out and have a look and if you still think we are in a shopping basket, by all means stay here.'

'Oh really!' said the Countess angrily. 'If you insist,

but I tell you we are in a shopping basket, going home.'

Boolar took the Countess's hand and helped her out of the box. She said nothing as they passed the smelly old trainer, though she did huff in a knowing kind of way.

'You see,' said Boolar, pointing out the banana skin, 'we are not in a shopping basket.'

'Wrong,' said the Countess stubbornly. 'That's just the kind of thing one might drop into a basket.'

As they reached the rim of the bin, the evening sun was shining down on them in lazy puddles of gold. Boolar could see Mr Mouse down on the path waving frantically.

'I need my umbrella,' said the Countess crossly. 'The sun's not good for my face.'

As she spoke, the sky above them went
black and there was a roar like thunder.

'*Three blind mice...*'

The park keeper's ugly moustached
face was almost on top of them.

In that split second, there was
a sudden whooshing of wings
as the brave old carrier pigeon

flew into the
park keeper's
face, before
picking up the
Countess and
flying off with her.

Boolar, taken completely by surprise, lost his balance and fell to the ground. He landed with a bump and was immediately pulled under the bushes by Mr Mouse. He couldn't see the Countess anywhere.

The park keeper was not sure what had just happened. It seemed to have something to do with a pigeon and a doll or two. He stood in the fading sunlight scratching the top of his head.

'Where is that Mr Cuddles when I need him?' he said.

Mr Mouse bolted the front door. 'That was a close squeak,' he said, taking out a large spotted hanky and mopping his brow.

'I should have made the Countess jump,'

said Boolar sadly. 'Then perhaps she'd
be here now.'

'Try not to think about it,' said Mr Mouse,
patting Boolar on the back. 'You did your
best. No one could have done more.
I'm sure it'll be all right in the end.'

They went down the hall to join the
others in the kitchen. Mrs Mouse had
put out some little cakes and the kettle
was humming happily on the stove

ready for tea.

'I think, my ribbly rodent, we are all in need of something a little stronger,' said Mr Mouse, going over to a corner cupboard and taking out six glasses and a bottle of elderflower wine. He poured out a drink for everyone.

'Thank you,' said Quilt, raising his glass. 'To Mr and Mrs Mouse for saving us.'

'We mustn't forget the Countess,' whispered Ting Tang.

They raised their glasses. 'To the bravery of Mr and Mr Mouse!' they shouted.

'Oh, it was nothing,' said Mr Mouse, looking bashful. He put his arm round his wife. 'We're a good team,' he said, giving her a little a kiss. 'We have been for years now.' Mrs Mouse blushed.

'What I would like to know,' said Ting Tang,

'is how you knew where we were.'

'The bees pass on all news,' said Mrs Mouse. 'The trouble was they told us you were going home with a little girl. Then, later, they came back to tell us you were in the rubbish bin.'

'If we'd known earlier,' said Mr Mouse, 'we might have been able to organise a proper rescue. Instead, it was very much a last minute thing.'

'I wonder what's happened to the Countess,' said Stitch.

'Well,' said Mr Mouse, 'this park

is a place of rhyme and riddle, I'm sure
she'll turn up.'

Stitch yawned. 'I'm very tired,' he said.
'Would it be all right if I went to bed?'

Mrs Mouse laughed. 'Of course. It's
been a long day.'

Ting Tang took Stitch down the corridor
to the bedroom and helped him to
undress. The minute his head touched
the soft feather pillow, he was fast asleep.

chapter seven

Boolar and Mr Mouse went out to collect
more wood for the fire while the others
helped Mrs Mouse get supper ready. It
was a fine evening and the park looked
still and peaceful. They were just about to
carry in the basket when through the
bushes came a very smartly dressed young
mouse wearing a trilby hat.

  Mr Mouse was delighted
to see his nephew. 'Ernst!
How are you?' he enquired.

  Ernst shrugged his shoulders.
'OK,' he said, 'until I got
lumbered with this.' He
pointed towards the bushes.
There was the Countess looking
a little worse for wear.

Boolar ran up to her.
'Are you all right?'
he asked anxiously.
'What do you mean?'
she snapped. 'How can you
possibly think I'm all right.'
'Well, you are safe. That's the
main thing,' said Boolar.
'Oh, really,' said the Countess.
'Look at my dress! It's ruined, and so is
my hair.'

'Are you sure, Uncle, that you want her
back?' said Ernst. 'Quite honestly, I think
the rubbish bin is the best place for her.'

The Countess poked at him with her
broken umbrella.

'Now, now,' said Mr Mouse. 'Let's go in
and tell the others the good news.'

Everyone let out a cry of joy when they

saw the Countess enter the kitchen.

'Oh, it's so good to see you,'
cried Ting Tang, rushing over to her.
'We've been so worried.'

'Tell us what happened and where you
have been,' said Quilt, helping the Countess
to a seat. She sat there stiff and cross.

'I was dropped from a great height into
a bush,' she said, 'and I had to wait ages
before that mouse brought me here.' She
poked Ernst once more with her umbrella.

'How come?' said Mr Mouse.

'Because I had to get ready. Tonight is a big night for me, Uncle. I need to look my best,' said Ernst, sitting down and pouring himself a drink.

'No,' said Mr Mouse. 'I mean how did you find the Countess?'

'Oh,' said Ernst. 'Really it was nothing to do with me. All the hard work was done by that old carrier pigeon who lives near the fountain.'

'Yes,' said Mrs Mouse. 'We asked him to help.'

'He arrived just in time,' said Ernst. 'He lifted her up into the air and out of danger just before the park keeper

caught her. I found
her beside the path.'

'I ask you!' interrupted the Countess.
'An old pigeon. You should have seen the
state of his claws. I mean, don't they have
any pride?'

Ernst took a swig of his elderflower wine.
'She poked and prodded the poor old bird
so many times with that umbrella of hers,
it's amazing he managed to cling on to
her at all.'

'Well, she's back safe and sound and
that's what matters,' said Mrs Mouse,
bringing a steaming hot pie to the table.
'Supper is ready.'

'Quite honestly, Uncle,' said Ernst,
'I would get rid of her sharpish. She is

nothing but trouble. And she's all airs and graces as if she were someone important.'

'I am,' said the Countess. 'Let me tell you, young man, I come from the Land of Lounge.'

'Yes, yes,' interrupted Ernst, getting up to go. 'So you've told me about a hundred times already.'

'Please stay and have supper with us,' said Mrs Mouse encouragingly. 'We'll all feel better after we've eaten.'

Ernst put his hat back on and gave Mrs Mouse a kiss on the cheek. 'That smells good, Auntie. Sorry I can't stay but I'm taking my girl out tonight, it's her birthday and I have bought her this,' he said, taking an engagement ring from his pocket. What do you think of it?'

Mrs Mouse hugged him.

'Oh, Ernst it's lovely,
she will be pleased.'

Mr Mouse patted him on the back.
'Not long until we have the engagement
party,' he said cheerfully.

'Are you sure, Auntie, it's all right to have
it here?' said Ernst. 'I mean, it won't be
too much trouble?'

Mrs Mouse laughed. 'Trouble to throw a
party for my favourite nephew? Not at all.'

'Before you go, Ernst, I would just like to thank you for your kindness,' said Boolar, 'and sorry for all the inconvenience.'

'It's not your fault,' said Ernst.

'Thank you,' said Quilt, shaking Ernst's hand.

'Yes, thank you very much,' said Ting Tang, giving him a kiss on the cheek.

'It was nothing,' said Ernst, looking pleased with himself. 'Glad I could be of help.'

'Good luck,' they called after him.

The dolls turned to look at the Countess who sat there with her china head held high.

They felt ashamed of her.

'You don't expect me to eat in this state, do you?' she said. 'I need a bath, warm towels, a change of dress.' She paused and thought for a moment, then added, 'Perhaps a cucumber sandwich with a touch of salt and vinegar might be nice.'

Boolar looked straight at her. 'You didn't even thank Ernst. It makes you look so spoiled.'

'Do I have to remind you who I am?' she said coldly. 'I am the Countess.'

'Which means nothing at all,' said Boolar.
'We are all merely dolls who have been left
in a box. But for the courage of Mr and
Mrs Mouse here, their nephew Ernst, and
the help of a bruised and battered pigeon,
we would now all be in a rubbish bin.'

'We weren't in a rubbish bin,' snapped
the Countess. 'Everyone knows we were
in a shopping basket about to go home.'
She stood up.

Mrs Mouse went over and gently took her
arm. 'You are tired and hungry, my dear.
Have a little pie and I will run you a bath
and lend you a nightie. How about that?'

The Countess sat down again.
'Thank you,' she muttered.

chapter eight

The next day, Mr Mouse decide it would be a good idea if Boolar and Quilt learnt how to collect food – a most important lesson if they were going to survive park life. The sun was shining and legs large and small were out enjoying themselves, drinking coffee at the café, eating waffles, and watching the painted horses on the merry-go-round go up and down. The three friends slipped from bush to bush, keeping out of sight as they looked for food.

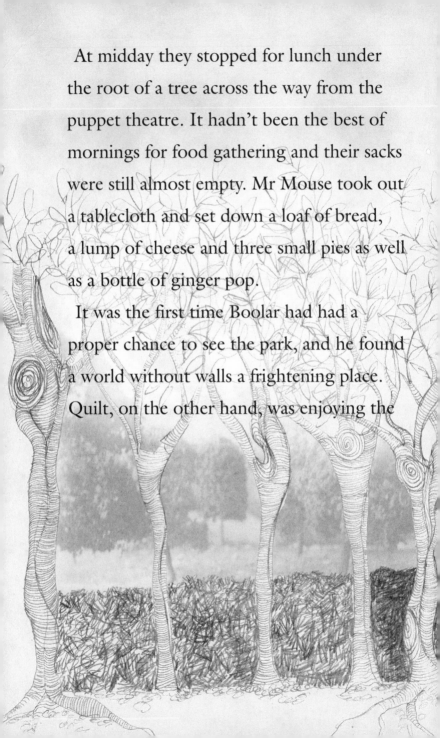

At midday they stopped for lunch under
the root of a tree across the way from the
puppet theatre. It hadn't been the best of
mornings for food gathering and their sacks
were still almost empty. Mr Mouse took out
a tablecloth and set down a loaf of bread,
a lump of cheese and three small pies as well
as a bottle of ginger pop.

It was the first time Boolar had had a
proper chance to see the park, and he found
a world without walls a frightening place.
Quilt, on the other hand, was enjoying the

open space. 'It's like a sea without end,' he declared.

They had just finished eating when the doors of the theatre opened and little and larger legs scattered out in every direction. 'Now,' said Mr Mouse, brushing the crumbs from his waistcoat, 'watch me carefully.' He ran through the legs on the tips of his paws, darting from side to side, and managed to bring back a pile of goodies without being seen.

'Listen,' said Mr Mouse, wiping his forehead with his hanky, 'whatever you do, you mustn't go into the theatre.'

'Why not?' asked Quilt.

'Let's just say I had a small disagreement with the puppets,' said Mr Mouse, looking embarrassed.

But Boolar was not paying attention. He couldn't take his eyes off the open door of the theatre. It was as if invisible strings were pulling at him and, without knowing why, he darted out into the courtyard in front of the theatre. Mr Mouse and Quilt watched open-mouthed as Boolar disappeared inside.

chapter nine

The curtains in the theatre were up
and the lights were still on. Before him,
Boolar saw a magical painted forest.
Without thinking twice, he climbed up
on to the stage. He stood for a moment,
taking it all in, then opening
his arms wide he said out
loud, 'Is this home?'

'I don't know about you,
old chap, but it's
my home all right,' said
a growly voice behind him.
Boolar spun round to see a huge beast
coming towards him. It had yellow eyes,
pointy ears, a pointy nose, and large sharp
white teeth that glistened. Boolar
remembered the Countess saying that

a huge cat had tried to
snatch her while she
was in the box, and
his heart jumped.
This is going to be the
end of me and there is
nothing I can do about it, he
thought. As Boolar stared, all
his fear slipped away. He could see now that
it was only a puppet.

'As in *The Three Little Pigs*,' explained
Mr Wolf. 'I'll huff and I'll puff and I'll
blow your house down,' and he roared
obligingly to show how it was done.

'Very good,' said Boolar, clapping.

'Didn't mean to frighten you, old chap,'
said the wolf kindly. 'I'm supposed to be
scary. It's part of the job description.'
He smiled. 'And who might you be?'

'My name is Boolar, and I was left in a box in the park with four other dolls,' he explained.

'Of course. I heard all about the great escape yesterday,' said Mr Wolf. 'You were lucky to get out of there in one piece.'

'It was down to Mr and Mrs Mouse,' said Boolar, 'that we were rescued at all, but unfortunately we lost our box.'

'And a jolly good box it is, too,' said Mr Wolf, 'made of wood with a well fitting lid, the sort of box that can keep you warm and dry.'

'How do you know?' asked Boolar, astonished.

'Because, old chap, I came across it the other evening when I tried to help that china doll. It was hopeless. She ran here, she ran there. I couldn't get any sense out of her.'

'The Countess said she'd seen a cat.'
Mr Wolf looked offended, and Boolar realised
he had said the wrong thing.

'Me? A cat!' said Mr Wolf. 'I don't think so.'

'You must forgive her. She has only ever
lived in the Land of Lounge,' explained
Boolar, 'so she doesn't know anything about
life in the big outside.'

'Quite so,' said Mr Wolf dryly. 'Anyway I
rescued your box from the rubbish when that
park keeper went to fetch his dreadful cat,
Mr Cuddles, and I put it back under the bush.'

The box! Boolar was lost for words. This
was turning out to be a wonderful day, full of
twists and surprises. He was enjoying himself
so much he quite forgot his friends waiting
anxiously outside.

chapter ten

By the time Boolar came out of the
stage door, it had started to rain.

The park was empty. All the legs had
gone home. Quilt and Mr Mouse
were sheltering under a large leaf,
trying to keep dry.

'What have you been doing?' said Mr Mouse.
'We have been very worried.'

'I'm sorry,' said Boolar, 'but the puppets
invited me in and showed me the theatre.
They gave me this,' he said,
excitedly pointing to a bag
full of food, 'and they
told me they had
rescued our box.'

'Oh, wonderful,'
said Quilt.

'Didn't they tell you to leave and never to darken their door again?' said Mr Mouse, looking puzzled.

'No,' said Boolar, equally puzzled by Mr Mouse's remark. 'They were very friendly. It's all over the park. Everyone knows how brave you were in rescuing us. The puppets said you were welcome back into the theatre any time.'

'Really?' said Mr Mouse. 'Well, twist my tail, that's good. What did I tell you? This park certainly is a place of rhyme and riddle.' He took Boolar by the arm. 'Come on, we'd better get home before the love of my whiskers starts to fret.'

The little band of food-gatherers arrived back to find Mrs Mouse in tears.

It seemed the Countess had told her that she wasn't wanted in her box.

'I can't repeat what she said to me,'
said Mrs Mouse, sobbing. 'It's too nasty
for your velvet ears to hear.'

'After all we've done for them,' said
Mr Mouse, bristling with anger.

'Please,' said Boolar, politely handing his
sack of food to Mrs Mouse. 'I'm sure it's
a silly misunderstanding. I'll sort it out.'

'Very well,' said Mr Mouse, 'but you can
tell her from me she will not be welcome
in our home, until she has said sorry.'

chapter eleven

The Countess, who had thought nothing
of taking one of Mrs Mouse's chairs and
a lamp without asking, was now sitting in
the middle of the box, looking like a bad-
tempered queen with the lamp beside her.
Stitch was standing in the corner with a
large top hat on his head and Ting Tang
was washing clothes in a bucket of water.

'What do you think you are doing?'
askd Boolar.

'Sitting,' said the Countess.
'It is very tiring being a mother.'

'Whose mother are you?'
asked Quilt, looking puzzled.

'I am Stitch's mother of course,'
she said sternly, 'and Boolar,
you are his father. Now, Father, Stitch has

been a very naughty boy and tried to give my hat away to that thieving Mrs Mouse. I've put him in the corner and told him you will be very cross with him when you get home.'

'Stop! Stop this,' shouted Boolar angrily. 'I'm not Stitch's father, and you are not Stitch's mother. We had never seen each other before we were put in the box.'

'Of course we hadn't,' said the Countess looking haughty. 'We are playing *let's pretend*, silly.'

'Those are the games children played with us,' said Quilt. 'They mean nothing now we are on our own.'

Quilt went over to Ting Tang who was still washing. 'Don't do that,' he said gently. 'You will ruin your hands. They are only made of cloth.'

'Leave her,' commanded the Countess. 'She is my *Hand Made* and will do what I say.'

'Your what?' said Boolar, disgusted.

'*My Hand Made,*' repeated the Countess. 'Come here and show Boolar.'

Ting Tang sadly lifted the corner of her dress. In pretty violet writing it said *Hand Made*.

'Now show Boolar *my* label,' the Countess ordered. Ting Tang fetched the Countess's dripping dress. The label said: *Wash separately. Delicate.* 'You see!' said the Countess. 'I am *delicate.*'

'The strong should look after the weak,' said Quilt. 'Ting Tang and Stitch are only made of cloth. The rest of us are made of sterner stuff.'

'If she's not my mother, can I stop
standing in the corner?' asked Stitch miserably.

'Yes,' said Boolar.

'No,' said the Countess firmly.

'Why do you have to be so unkind
to everyone? Do you have no heart?'
asked Boolar.

'Of course I don't,' said the Countess.
'I am far too important.'

Quilt helped Ting Tang out of the box.
'Come on, let's see if Mrs Mouse will have
us back in, then you will be able to dry
out those wet hands by a warm fire,' he said.

When they had gone, Boolar went over
to the hat that Mrs Mouse had fancied.

'Leave that,' shouted the Countess,
'it's mine.'

'Listen to me. Without Mr and Mrs Mouse
we would all have been lifeless long ago.

We should be grateful to them. All you do is upset everyone. What makes *you* so special?' said Boolar.

'I am wanted!' shouted the Countess. 'A beautiful little girl used to play with me. And do you know what she would say? She'd look at me and whisper, "I wish I had a mother like you." '

Boolar looked at her hard. 'I will take the chair and lamp with me. They don't belong to you.'

'And what am I supposed to do? Just stand here?'

'I don't mind, and I don't care,' said Boolar. 'Perhaps when you come to Mrs Mouse for supper you could bring this hat as a gift for her and say you are very sorry for all your rudeness.'

The Countess was left alone in the box, surrounded by clothes that didn't fit.

'I would rather stay here for ever,' she said to the darkness, 'than give one of my hats to a mere mouse.'

chapter twelve

The days that followed were difficult ones for the dolls. The Countess did not come to say sorry to Mrs Mouse. Instead, she took to standing on top of the box, then climbing down and pushing it with all her might away from Mr and Mrs Mouse's house.

No one knew what she was trying to do, though many in the park watched her with interest, especially Mr Cuddles.

It was Ting Tang who decided to go and talk to her since no one else would.

She couldn't bear the bad feelings that had settled over them all like sticky dust.

She found the Countess on top of the box as usual.

'I don't think it's safe you being out here on your own,' said Ting Tang.

'Go away! You are of no importance,' said the Countess.

Ting Tang continued bravely, 'Mr Mouse says that Mr Cuddles has his eye on you and that you are in great danger.'

'Fiddlesticks,' said the Countess. 'What would a doll made out of cloth know about anything?' She adjusted her hat. 'I am far

too important
to be bothered
by a mangy cat.'
Ting Tang
walked over

to the ladder that the Countess
had left propped up against the side
of the box.

'We should try to stay together, don't
you think?' she said, beginning to climb
up. 'Please come back, I will be your
Hand Made if that will make you happy.
I don't mind, honestly I don't.'

The Countess looked down at her.
'I don't need you. What use is a *Hand
Made* without proper feet or hands?'

Ting Tang felt as though she had been
pierced with an arrow. She climbed down
the ladder and, without another word,

went back inside Mr and Mrs Mouse's house. She sat sadly on her little bed. The Countess was right, she thought. I don't have proper feet or hands like the other dolls. They are beautiful and special. I am soft and have no proper shape. A *Hand Made* with no fingers.

chapter thirteen

That night, Mr and Mrs Mouse and
the dolls were woken by a terrible noise
from the great outside. A thunderous
purring was making the little front
door rattle.

'We should see what's happening,'
said Ting Tang. 'The Countess
could be in terrible trouble.'

'It's no good my dear friends,'
said Mr Mouse, 'there's nothing
we can do. If it is Mr Cuddles
outside he would gobble us up.'

Mrs Mouse let out a squeak.
'No one must go outside, it would
be the end of us,' she said shakily.
'Much better to wait until morning.'

 Ting Tang and the
others went back to
their beds. Ting Tang lay there, unable
to sleep. She couldn't stop thinking about
the Countess out there in the box all alone.

The next morning bright and early, Ernst
came round, to tell them he had just seen
the Countess tied to the front of the park
keeper's cart.

'Oh dear,' said Mr Mouse. 'I'm afraid
what we heard last night was the Countess
being captured by Mr Cuddles.'

'Good riddance to bad rubbish,'
said Ernst, helping himself
to a hot buttered roll.
'She won't last a day,'
said Mr Mouse, looking
out of the kitchen window,
'not in this wind.'

All the dolls were very quiet. It is one thing to say you would like to see the end of someone, and quite another when it happens.

'Oh, I nearly forgot,' said Ernst, getting up and wiping his whiskers, 'I found this on my way here. I thought you might like to keep it as a souvenir.' He went into the hall and came back with one of the Countess's arms.

Ting Tang let out a scream.

'Ernst!' said Mr Mouse, 'not when we are eating.'

'Sorry, Uncle,' said Ernst, taking the arm off the kitchen table and propping it up in the corner of the room.

Seeing the arm was almost too much
to bear. Ting Tang said in a shaky voice,
'I know I'm only made of cloth and am
of no importance because I don't have
proper feet and hands like all of you, but
I feel if we lose one of us then we're all lost.'

'What are you saying?' said Boolar.

'That we should rescue the Countess, even
though she has said and done things we
don't like, because we all belong together
no matter what,' said Ting Tang shyly.

'Why?' said Stitch? 'She was horrible
to you and she was a nasty mother to me.'

'I think Ting Tang's got a point,' said Quilt.

'Sorry,' said Ernst, 'I'm missing something.
You aren't going to try and rescue that
snotty dotty doll, are you?'

'You really are better off without her,' said
Mr Mouse gently. 'Now she's out of the box,
we can help you make it into a fine home.'

Mr Mouse looked at the sad faces of the dolls and tried, as kindly as he could, to tell them that no toy lasted long on the cart. 'It's as good as being swallowed by a dragon,' he said.

'Anyway,' said Ernst, wiping his mouth, 'no one can do anything until this wind has died down.'

Everyone started talking about whether or not to rescue the Countess. They were all so busy that no one noticed Ting Tang slip away from the breakfast table and out of the front door.

chapter fourteen

As Ting Tang closed the front door, she
was not sure what she was going to do, or
which way to go. A gust of wind billowed
out her skirts, lifted her for a moment off
her feet, twirled her round, and put her
down again. Ting Tang, who had spent
her whole life indoors, had never met
a strong wind before. It seemed to
know which way she should go.
She found herself being
propelled along from one bush
to another, the leaves dancing
and spinning around her.

Ting Tang allowed the wind to take her,
until she saw the park keeper's cart
wobbling along the gravel path towards
her. Mr Cuddles was walking in front,
his tail held high.

  She waited until Mr Cuddles had gone
past, and the cart was very near her and
she ran and jumped as high as she could.
At that moment, a gust of wind blew
and to her surprise she found she had

landed on a very lifeless bear that was tied
to the cart. Ting Tang climbed carefully
over the other sad and lost toys until she
saw the Countess. She was in a sorry state.
Her face was chipped and her stuffing was
coming out. Her arm was missing and one
of her legs was broken. There was a sharp
jagged edge where her foot had been.

'Is that you, Ting Tang?'
said the Countess in a weak voice.

'Yes,' said Ting Tang, trying
to free the Countess from
a twist of wire that was
holding her down.

'I'm here to rescue you.'

It was hard with only cloth
hands to untwist the wire,
and it seemed to be taking
a long time.

'Oh, Ting Tang.
Where are the others?'
asked the Countess.

'I expect they will be along
shortly. There!' said Ting Tang
with pride. 'I've done it.'
'Look out!' shouted the Countess.
It was too late. The large rough
hand of the park keeper grabbed
hold of Ting Tang and held her
in the air.
'What have we got here?' he said.
'Well, well. If it isn't a sweet little
doll and not a mark on her.'

'She's mine,' purred Mr Cuddles.
'Give her to me.' He sidled up against
the park keeper's legs. 'Come on,
drop her,' he purred roughly.

'No,' said the park keeper. 'You're not
getting your paws on this one. She's
special.' He smiled to himself and
wrapped Ting Tang tightly in his hanky
before slipping her into his coat pocket.

Mr Cuddles was not in a good mood
as they started for home. His tail swished
angrily back and forth.

The keeper, on the other hand, pleased with his find, started singing merrily away to himself. The cart wobbled along the path until suddenly, the Countess, who Ting Tang had freed from the wire, was thrown clear. She landed in a puddle. As the cart rolled away, she managed to pull herself out of the muddy water, and lay on the gravel like a scrunched-up piece of rubbish.

chapter fifteen

It was the time of half light and shadows
when Mr and Mrs Mouse, Boolar, Quilt,
and Stitch set off in search of the Countess
and Ting Tang.

The news from the bees was not good.
Ting Tang had last been seen high above
the park being blown hither and thither
by the wind. The Countess had been tied
to the front of the park keeper's cart.

They walked in single file, armed with
walking sticks, umbrellas and saucepans,
staying as close to the bushes as they could.

Stitch was doing his best to keep up with
Mrs Mouse when he fell over. 'Ow!' he cried.

'Sshh,' said the others.

'But I've hurt myself. I've tripped over
a piece of rubbish and it's got something
sharp in it.'

Mrs Mouse was helping him up when the
piece of rubbish spoke.

'Is that you, Boolar?' it said in a whisper.

'Oh my,' said Mr Mouse, bending down to
take a closer look. 'It's the Countess.'

'She's injured,' said Boolar.

'We must get her back to the box.'

They lifted her as carefully as they could but her sawdust stuffing kept seeping out.

'I can't bear to look,' said Stitch. 'She's lost an arm and most of her leg.'

Mrs Mouse took off her scarf and wrapped it round the Countess but still the sawdust seeped out onto the ground.

'Go home,' said the Countess weakly, 'before that man catches you. There's nothing you can do for me.'

Mr Mouse scratched his ear. This was a pretty pickle and no mistake.

'The love of my whiskers,' he said, taking Mrs Mouse's hand, 'I think we need help. Take Stitch and go and tell the puppets we are in trouble.'

'The puppets, my love,' she said. 'Are you sure?'

'Yes, my ribbly rodent, there's not a whisker to lose.'

They watched as Mrs Mouse and Stitch disappeared into the gathering gloom.

'All we can do is wait and hope,' said Mr Mouse bravely as they tried to drag the Countess to safety. It was no good.

It looked as if her remaining arm might fall off. They sat down on the gravel path beside her, hoping no cats would be out on the prowl.

chapter sixteen

Mr Cuddles had turned up his
nose at supper. He made his way
back out into the park. His tummy
was rumbling and he felt very angry.
That should have been his doll to tear to
pieces as he pleased. He stopped to sharpen
his claws on a tree. It was a cool evening and
his eyes, as yellow as torches, helped him to
see in the dark. He liked what he saw. On
the path up ahead were two dolls and one
deliciously fat little mouse. Let the keeper
have his doll, thought Mr Cuddles. Here
was food and enough entertainment to last
the night. He crept nearer and nearer, his
tail waving silently from side to side, his
shape hidden in the darkness. He reached
the group and pounced!

He caught Boolar by his
jacket and tossed him
into the air. Boolar
fought back with all
his strength.

The idea of
a doll with a
stick amused
Mr Cuddles.
He was about to bring
his paw down on top of
Boolar when Mr Mouse
rushed forward, charging the cat
with his umbrella. Quilt watched in horror
as Mr Cuddles' paw came down on
Mr Mouse's tail. He was pinned to
the spot, unable to move.

Mr Cuddles ran his sharp claws across
Mr Mouse's fat roly-poly tummy.

'Purr,' went Mr Cuddles. 'Mmmm.'
With a wicked gleam in his eye, he let
the mouse go.

Mr Mouse began to run for his life.
Once again, the paw came down hard
on his tail, stopping him in his tracks.
Mr Cuddles licked his lips. 'What a
tasty morsel!' he gloated. Boolar was
up again, ready to do battle, and so
was Quilt. They were about to
go at the cat
with the
saucepan when,
to their astonishment,
the Countess stood up,
sawdust pouring from her
body. She brought her
jagged china leg down
on Mr Cuddles' paw.

The effect was immediate. The huge cat arched his back and hissed before running away, dragging his paw behind him.

'Yes!' shouted Quilt. 'You did it!'
The Countess smiled weakly, then fell to the ground in a heap. Quilt tried to pick her up but it was no good. She lay there, lifeless. Quilt and Mr Mouse knelt beside her.

'Countess,' said Quilt, patting her hand, 'talk to me.'

The three friends were wondering what to do next when out of the darkness came a voice that Boolar knew.

chapter seventeen

'Having a spot of trouble,
old chap?' It was Mr Wolf.
He carefully picked up
the Countess, and
wound his hanky around
her so no more stuffing
would fall out. 'I should
get you three home first,'
he said, escorting them
to Mr Mouse's front door.
'Then we'll see about
the Countess.'

Mrs Mouse and Stitch
were so pleased to see them.

'Will the Countess be all
right?' asked Boolar

as Mr Wolf was about to leave.

'I don't know,' said Mr Wolf.
'We will have to see what the puppet
master can do. He has a magic way with
dolls; if anyone can put her back together,
old chap, then he's your man.'

'Wait a minute,' said Boolar, going inside
and coming out again with the Countess's
arm. 'You'll need this.'

'Don't get your hopes up,
old chap,' said Mr Wolf,
patting Boolar gently on the
back. 'It doesn't look good.'
And he turned and
walked away
towards the theatre.

chapter eighteen

The puppet master had worked at the theatre for many years and knew it to be a place of magic and mystery. He had brought many a puppet to life and wasn't in the least surprised to find a broken doll on his workbench the next morning.

He looked carefully at the crumpled Countess, and said, 'Poor old lady, what happened to you? Looks like you've been in the wars.'

He had to use all his skill to restore the her. First, the puppet master gently washed the mud away to see what kind of doll she was.

As he suspected, he found her to be very old and very precious, but limp through the loss of her sawdust.

The puppet master made her a beautiful little heart with beads on it. He put it carefully in her chest, surrounded it with soft cotton stuffing and sewed her up again. After each repair, he left her to recover on a small bed, wrapped up in a warm blanket. The broken leg with the missing foot proved more difficult to mend and, in the end, he decided to take the leg off and put a new one on. It didn't quite match but at least it would be strong. The arm went on

with no trouble at all.
Next, he tied and added
more red hair, which he
twisted and pinned up.
Then he painted and mended her
face, putting a smile on her lips and
a twinkle in her eye.

'All you need now, my lady,' said the
puppet master, 'are some new clothes.'
He found her a yellow dress that fitted
as if it had been made for her
and some red shoes.
When he was quite
satisfied, he sat her
down on the workbench
and looked at her. He
had done a good job.

'I wonder if you will be here tomorrow?' he said to her before closing the workshop door.

The Countess stirred at his words and realised to her delight that she was no longer fading away. When she was sure he had gone, she stood up and moved her arms and legs, expecting to be her usual hard, stiff self. Imagine her surprise to find she could move easily. She could even touch her toes. Then she did something she couldn't remember ever doing before. She danced!

Just at that moment, the workshop door was pushed quietly open. The Countess stopped dancing and stood very still.

'Glad to see you up again,' said Mr Wolf.

'We have all been most worried about you.'

The Countess looked at Mr Wolf coming into the workshop, and wondered how she could have mistaken this kind fellow for Mr Cuddles. 'Have I been here long?' she said.

'Only a week,' said Mr Wolf, 'which is good when you think how badly hurt you were.'

'Are Mr and Mrs Mouse and the dolls safe?' asked the Countess.

'All apart from Ting Tang. No one has seen her since the day you were caught. I am afraid we think she is lost,' said Mr Wolf.

'It's all my fault,' said the Countess.
'If I hadn't—'

Mr Wolf interrupted. 'Don't cry,
for, if you do, your new paint will run.'

The Countess told Mr Wolf all she
could remember about Ting Tang
and how she had seen her being put
in the keeper's pocket.

Mr Wolf thought for a moment,
then he asked the Countess, 'Are you willing
to help me? It may be dangerous.'

'Yes,' she replied, 'but first I must leave
a note.' Taking a pencil from the jar, the
Countess wrote in beautiful handwriting,
for the puppet master to see:
'*I thank you, from the bottom
of my heart.*' And she signed it:
The Countess.

chapter nineteen

Mr Cuddles stayed curled up on his cushion. The Countess had hurt him so much that his paw was now in a bandage. He didn't want anyone seeing him like this. After all, *he* was the tiger of the park, a panther, not an ordinary cat with a sore paw.

Ting Tang had been placed on the mantelpiece. She had made several unsuccessful attempts to escape. All had ended with the park keeper picking her up and saying, 'Careful! We don't want Mr Cuddles to get you, do we my pretty?'

Ting Tang had no idea why the park keeper thought she was so special. Every time he looked at her, he would smile.

On the fourth day
of being on the shelf,
Ting Tang heard him
speaking to his daughter
on the phone. It took her a few moments
to realise he was talking about her.

'Do you remember that little doll you
had when you were small? You know, the
one Mum made for you. She sewed it all
by hand. Oh, the care she took with that
doll. She put her heart into it. When you
were a baby, it used to sit next to you and
when you left home, we put it in the glass
cupboard. That's right... You won't
believe it, but I found one almost the
same in the park.'

Listening to the park
keeper talk
brought back

all Ting Tang's lost memories. She had
been given to babies when they were
born, had sat with them in cots and cribs,
in prams and pushchairs, watched over
them while they slept. When each one
was older, she had been put out of harm's
way until the next baby came along.

If I had had real hands,
babies wouldn't have let
me stay in their cots, thought
Ting Tang. I would have been
too hard for their soft skin.
Her heart sang. She was special.
She had been handmade with love.

Mr Cuddle's was due for his last check-
up with the vet that afternoon. After
a great deal of fighting and scratching,
the park keeper managed to get hold
of him and put him in his cat basket.

Mr Cuddles meowed and hissed, but the keeper took no notice. 'It's got to be done,' he said as he left.

Ting Tang was wondering how best to make her escape when, to her surprise, through the open window came a pointy nose and sharp white teeth. Oh dear, she thought, this is worse than Mr Cuddles. This is a beast.

Mr Wolf opened the window a little farther and placed the Countess on the windowsill. 'Can you see her?' he whispered.

The Countess jumped
down onto the kitchen
table and looked round.
Ting Tang couldn't
believe her eyes. Was this lovely
lady doll with the smiling face really
the grumpy old Countess?

'Is that you?' she asked hopefully.

'Oh, Ting Tang, how wonderful!
You are all right. I've found her,
I found her!' shouted the Countess.
Mr Wolf had by now climbed
in too, and he helped Ting Tang
off the mantelpiece just in the nick
of time. The park keeper had forgotten
something. They could hear his key
turning in the front door, just as Mr Wolf
made his escape holding on tightly to
Ting Tang and the Countess.

Mr and Mrs Mouse were having the engagement party that evening for Ernst and his bride-to-be. Mr Mouse had fully recovered from his injury. Apart from the fact that his tail was crooked, you would never have known he had been in a battle with a cat.

It had been such an unhappy week for everyone. They were almost certain now that Ting Tang was lost for good and there had been no news from the bees or the puppets as to whether the Countess

had been mended or not.

'A party is the answer,' said Mr Mouse. 'Park life has to go on. It doesn't help us to mope around.'

They all did their best to get Ernst's engagement party ready. Mr Mouse and Quilt brought out tables which they joined together and spread with a huge cloth. All sorts of chairs were found, and Boolar hung strings of lanterns from the branches overhanging the little house.

'It looks a picture,' said Mrs Mouse who had spent the day cooking. There were so many dishes, Mr Mouse said they wouldn't need to go food-gathering for a fortnight. They all made the effort to dress up.

Ernst was the first to arrive with his fiancée. They were followed by relatives of all ages and sizes. Stitch was surprised to see that a tiny jointed bear had come along.

He told Boolar he lived with a family of mice over by the fountain, and that Stitch should come round for tea one day.

When they were all seated, Mr Mouse tapped his glass with a spoon.

'My friends, before we eat, I would like to propose a toast. To Ernst and Ermintrude, and to our absent friends.'

They all raised their glasses and thought mournfully of Ting Tang and the Countess.

The sad moment swiftly passed and soon everyone was eating and talking away and listening to a little band that had begun to play. Suddenly, the bushes parted and there was Mr Wolf.

'Good evening,' said Mr Mouse a little nervously. 'I am honoured to have such a great star as you at our humble little party.'

'It is very kind of you,' said Mr Wolf. 'I hope you don't mind but I've brought two friends along with me.'

'The more the merrier,' said Mrs Mouse.

There was a gasp of disbelief as Ting Tang stepped shyly forward from behind Mr Wolf. The dolls rose to greet her.

'Wait,' said Ting Tang. 'There's another surprise.' And she pointed to the bushes. Everyone was silent as the Countess emerged. But could this be the same grumpy old Countess? She went straight up to Mrs Mouse and said:

'I am very sorry I behaved so badly and was so unkind to you and everyone else.'

'It doesn't matter now. Just look at you!'

said Mrs Mouse, beaming.

'I know it's no excuse,' said the Countess, 'but I think my behaviour might have had something to do with my stuffing.'

Stitch rushed over and gave her a hug.

'She's right,' he said. 'She is all soft now!'

'You saved us from Mr Cuddles,'
said Boolar. 'Without you, we would
all have been lost.'

'You were so brave. It is wonderful
to have you back,' said Mr Mouse.

'Long live the Countess!' shouted Quilt.

'Hear, hear!' came the reply.

'Let the party begin,' said Mr Mouse.

Other Bloomsbury titles by the same author:
Polly's Running Away Book
Polly's Absolutely Worst Birthday Ever

And for Orion:
The Magical Children series